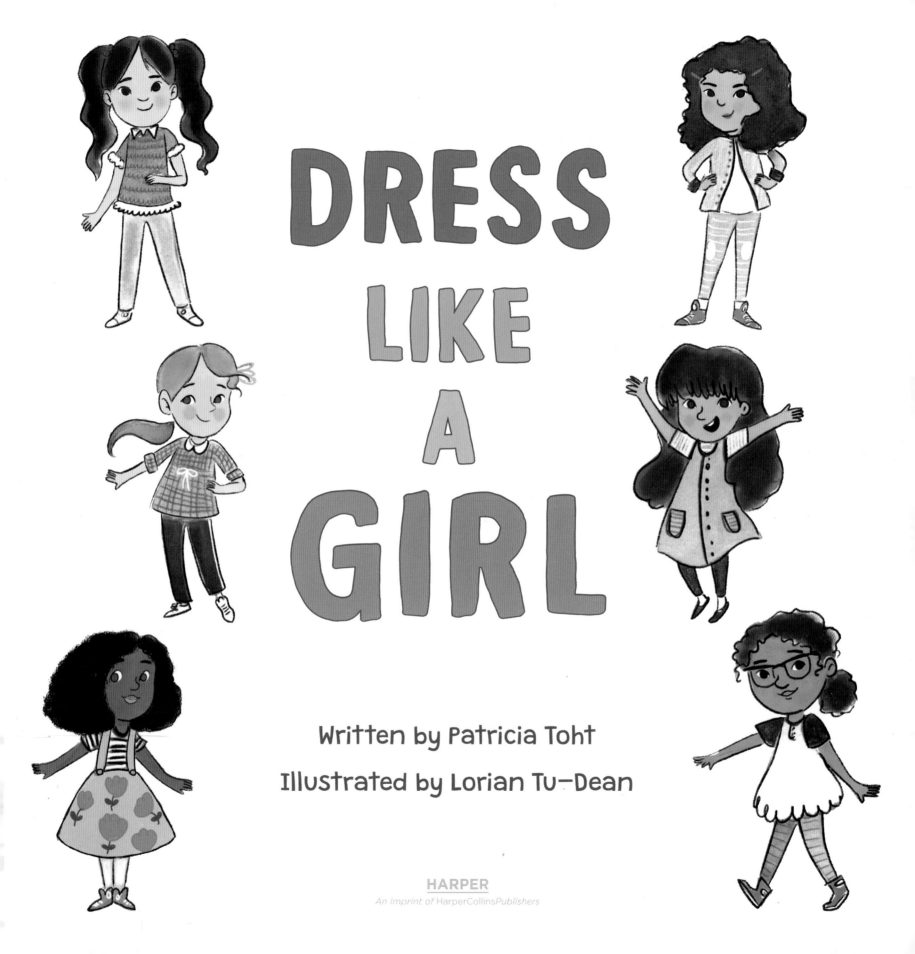

DRESS LIKE A GIRL

Written by Patricia Toht

Illustrated by Lorian Tu-Dean

HARPER

An Imprint of HarperCollinsPublishers

To Vivian
—P.T.

Para ti, Abuelita.
And for all the girls in my life,
especially Sadie and Stella.
—L.D.

Dress Like a Girl

Text copyright © 2019 by Patricia Toht

Illustrations copyright © 2019 by Lorian Tu-Dean

All rights reserved. Manufactured in China.

No part of this book may be used or reproduced in any manner whatsoever without written

permission except in the case of brief quotations embodied in critical articles and reviews.

For information address HarperCollins Children's Books, a division of HarperCollins Publishers,

195 Broadway, New York, NY 10007.

www.harpercollinschildrens.com

ISBN 978-0-06-279892-3

The artist used watercolor, gouache, colored pencil, and ink to create the digital illustrations

for this book.

Typography by Alison Klapthor

18 19 20 21 22   SCP   10 9 8 7 6 5 4 3 2 1

❖

First Edition

What does it mean to dress like a girl?

Many will tell you in this big wide world

that there are strict rules that must be addressed,

rules you will need when looking your best.

But when you are given these rules to obey,

the secret is heeding them—in *your own way*.

On hot summer days the look is crisp white,

on land or at sea or on a long flight.

White is a look you can manage with grace

as you soar in a rocket ship through outer space!

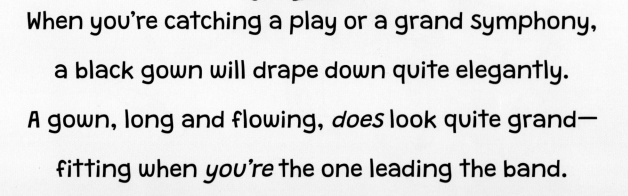

When you're catching a play or a grand symphony,

a black gown will drape down quite elegantly.

A gown, long and flowing, *does* look quite grand—

fitting when *you're* the one leading the band.

To make a strong statement
choose bright, vivid hues.
You can be brave dressed in
reds or in blues.

With patterns it's best to
be subtle, my friend.
Join a safari
and you'll be on trend.

Toting some trinkets? Deep pockets hold all.

Grab your white lab coat. The doctor's on call!

Sleek swimwear is best when you visit the shore.

Slip on some flippers. Explore the seafloor.

Arctic adventure!

It's twenty below!

Remember to always

dress warm in the snow.

It's game day!

So sport your team colors with pride.

Wear jerseys and helmets;

play hard for your side.

Pick a hat for your head

and chic Shoes for your feet.

Construct your best outfit—

a look that's complete.

Style calls for craftiness.

Fashion's an art!

Change up your clothing

to always look smart.

Express your true self, for there's only *one* you.

Can't find what you like? Then design something new!

What *you* think determines which outfit's okay.

Don't *judge* your appearance

by what others say.

Make your own rules

in this big wide world.

Set your sights high

and . . .

...DRESS LIKE A GIRL!

...DRESS LIKE A GIRL!